For the three Elizabeths:
Elizabeth Richardson Pulley, Catherine Elizabeth Pulley Ballard,
and Helen Elizabeth Ballard

—A. P. S.

To the memory of my father, home at last

—A. B.

Henry Holt and Company, LLC, *Publishers since 1866*
115 West 18th Street, New York, New York 10011

Henry Holt is a registered trademark of Henry Holt and Company, LLC
Text copyright © 1998 by April Pulley Sayre. Illustrations copyright © 1998 by Alix Berenzy
All rights reserved.
Distributed in Canada by H. B. Fenn and Company Ltd.

Library of Congress Cataloging-in-Publication Data
Sayre, April Pulley.
Home at last /April Pulley Sayre; illustrations by Alix Berenzy.
Summary: Describes how a variety of creatures, including a butterfly, a sea turtle,
a caribou herd, and an Arctic tern, find their ways home.
1. Animal migration—Juvenile literature. [1.Animals—Migration.] I. Berenzy, Alix, ill. II. Title.
QL754.S29 1998 591.56'8—dc21 97-11481

ISBN 0-8050-5154-6 / First Edition—1998
Designed by Martha Rago
The artist used soft pastel on black paper to create the illustrations for this book.
Printed in Hong Kong
3 5 7 9 10 8 6 4 2

Home at Last

A Song of Migration

April Pulley Sayre

ILLUSTRATIONS BY **Alix Berenzy**

Henry Holt and Company ∽ New York

In the dark of night, a warbler finds her way by stars. Her wings flap a thousand miles. Will she reach her summer home? No one knows. But like the others, she's heading for home at last.

Out at sea, grown-up salmon remember a smell. It's the smell of the stream where they were born. They'll swim two thousand miles. Hop up waterfalls. Just to be . . .

. . . home at last.

Flippers push, gently paddle. A sea turtle swims. No one knows how she finds her way. But she swims across the ocean to a beach where she was born. She lays her eggs there . . .

. . . home at last.

Tiny wings carry a monarch hundreds of miles. One flutter and flap at a time. She flies to a mountain she's never seen. Yet somehow she knows she's . . .

. . . home at last.

On his first journey, a young gray whale swims with his mother. From warm tropical waters to cold Arctic seas. Once there, he and his family will feast on plankton aplenty. Fat and full, they'll be . . .

. . . home at last.

A caribou herd, like a
river of antlers, walks
and eats and walks. They
head from the forest to
their summer home, the
coastal plain. When they
reach it, they'll be . . .

. . . home at last.

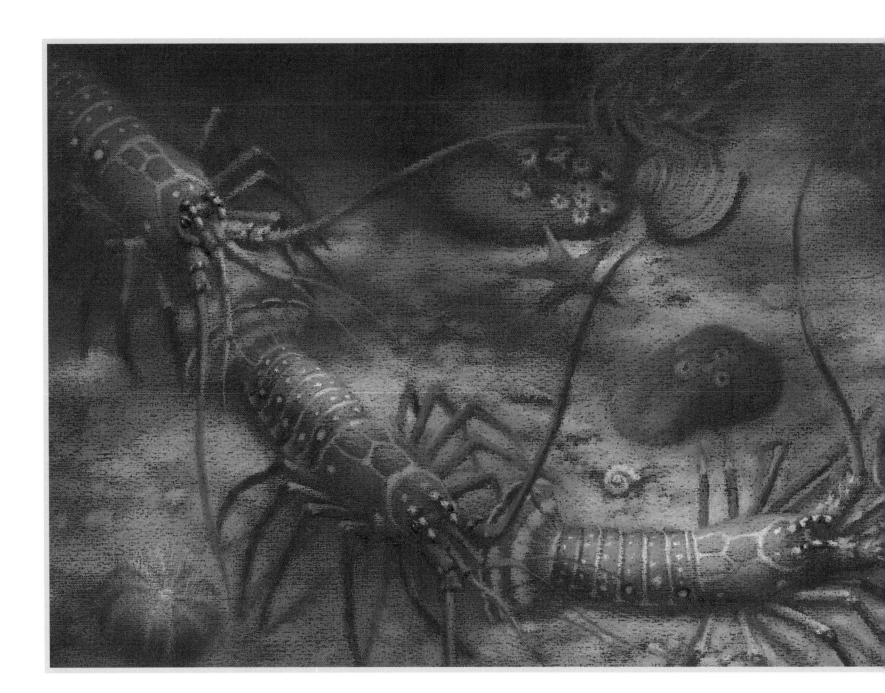

In fall, lobsters walk single file. From deep water to their winter home—the reef. March, march, march. Tentacle to tail. They march until they're . . .

. . . home at last.

An Arctic tern hovers, then dives for fish. He has two homes: one at each end of the earth. He'll need lots of food to fuel his twelve-thousand-mile trip. But it's worth it to be . . .

. . . home at last.

In spring, a wood frog hops. Over rocks. Through fields. Across roads. By a house. He smells the moist air. The leaves. The pond. And then he knows he's . . .

. . . home at last.

In that same pond, the frog joins a chorus. They fill the forest with sound. Just then, a tired bird lands on a branch high above.

The warbler has reached
her home. At last.

Yellow-Rumped Warbler

Each year, northern bird-watchers wait with excitement for the arrival of tiny, colorful birds—yellow-rumped warblers. These warblers are one of the first species to arrive in spring. Yellow-rumped warblers weigh only half an ounce and are five to six inches long from beak to tail. In winter, they live in the southern United States and in Central America. In spring, they fly north to other parts of the U.S. and Canada. To find its way, a warbler uses clues such as the position of the stars, landmarks, and the earth's magnetic field. Yet even after a long journey as far as six thousand miles, the warbler may build its nest in the very same tree as the year before.

Salmon

Weighing up to eighty pounds and stretching as long as five feet, salmon are big fish. Even bigger is their journey. After hatching in a river, young salmon swim downstream to the ocean. Once grown, they swim through the ocean, up rivers, and back into streams. Only when they find their home stream will they lay and fertilize their eggs.

Green Turtle

Green turtles are sea turtles that can be four feet long and weigh as much as four hundred pounds. But these sea creatures lay their eggs on land. When it is time, the females swim back to the beach where they were hatched. There, they crawl out of the ocean, dig a hole, and lay about a hundred eggs in a sandy nest. Sometimes a female turtle returns to a beach she has not seen for twenty years!

Monarch Butterfly

In fall, monarch butterflies from all over the United States and Canada fly southward to parts of California and Mexico. In winter, the trees in these places are covered with monarch butterflies. In spring, the monarchs fly northward once again, mating and laying eggs along the way. No single butterfly lives long enough to complete the round-trip journey, but several generations make the journey over time.

Gray Whale

Gray whales are some of the largest mammals in the world, reaching lengths of forty-five feet and weighing up to thirty-seven tons. Each spring, these whales migrate from warm waters near Baja, Mexico, to the

Arctic. Their round-trip journey is almost 12,500 miles. During this migration, gray whales often swim near the coastline, so many people are able to watch them along the west coast of the United States.

Caribou

Caribou, members of the deer family, stand up to four feet tall and weigh as much as four hundred pounds. Each year, hundreds of thousands of caribou migrate to Alaska from their wintering grounds in Canada. The trip is long—more than a thousand miles—and the caribou must cross rivers and escape hungry wolf packs. Female caribou always travel together, reaching the coastal plain of Alaska first, where they give birth to calves in summer.

Spiny Lobster

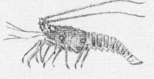

In ocean waters from North Carolina to Brazil, thousands of spiny lobsters migrate south in the fall. Spiny lobsters are up to sixteen inches long and do not have claws. During migration, spiny lobsters walk as far as nine miles a day, single file! Fifty or more may line up. They stay in line by touching their antennae to the lobster in front of them.

Arctic Tern

Arctic terns are graceful fish-eating birds that measure about sixteen inches long from beak to tail. Each year Arctic terns make one of the world's longest migratory journeys—more than twenty-four thousand miles round-trip. These birds raise their chicks in the Arctic in the summer. But when it gets cold, they fly all the way to Antarctica, where summer is just beginning. Because they go to both poles, they experience more summer and more daylight than any other animal on earth.

Wood Frog

Wood frogs are three-inch-long North American amphibians whose tadpoles hatch in ponds. Once the tadpoles develop into frogs, they hop far away into the countryside. Years later, as adults, the wood frogs migrate back to the pond where they were born in order to lay and fertilize their eggs. The frogs find their home pond partly by the way it smells.

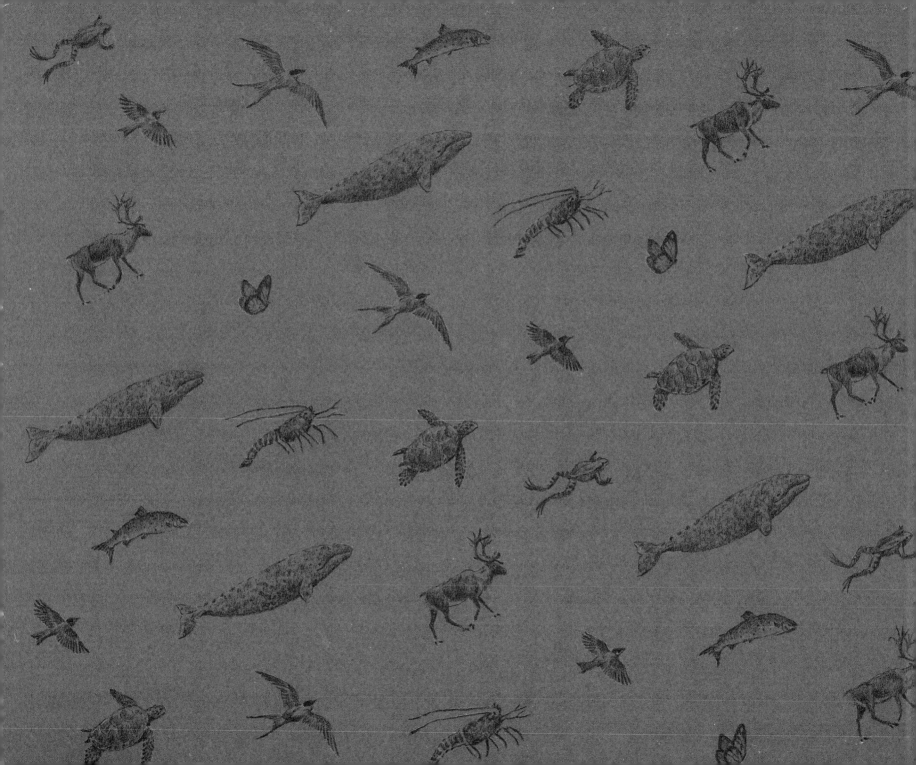